Turning, Joe leaped into the air.
He threw the ball hard.
It dropped through the net.

"Another two points, Wishbone!" Joe let the ball bounce once. Then he grabbed it. "That's five points in a row!"

"Not bad," said an unfamiliar voice.

Joe and Wishbone turned around.

Wishbone looked up. Two older boys walked onto the court. One of the boys was tall. The other one was even taller, almost a giant. He had a blue-and-red basketball tucked under his arm.

Whoa! Wishbone thought, as he saw the taller boy's shoes. *Look at the size of those sneakers!*

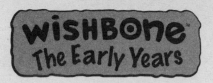

The Brave Little Tailor

The Brave Little Tailor

by Vivian Sathre

WISHBONE™ created by Rick Duffield

SCHOLASTIC INC.

New York Toronto London Auckland Sydney
Mexico City New Delhi Hong Kong

ISBN 0-439-12838-2

Copyright © 1999 by Big Feats Entertainment, L.P.
All rights reserved.
Published by Scholastic Inc., 555 Broadway, New York, NY 10012,
by arrangement with Lyrick Publishing™.
SCHOLASTIC and associated logos are trademarks
and/or registered trademarks of Scholastic Inc.
WISHBONE, the Wishbone portrait, and the Big Feats! Entertainment
logo are trademarks and service marks of Big Feats Entertainment, L.P.
WISHBONE is Reg. U.S. Pat. & Tm. Off.

12 11 10 9 8 7 6 5 4 3 2 1   0 1 2 3 4 5/0

Printed in the U.S.A.   40

First Scholastic printing, February 2000

Edited by Pam Pollack
Copy edited by Jonathon Brodman
Continuity editing by Grace Gantt
Cover design by Lyle Miller
Cover painting and interior illustrations by Kathryn Yingling

For Vicci, Vickie, and Stan,
with special thanks to Linda Collier
for her never-ending help

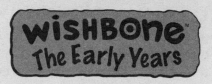

The Brave Little Tailor

A WORD FROM OUR TOP DOG . . .

Helllooo! Wishbone here. Welcome to my
brand-new series of books, Wishbone: The Early Years.
These books tell the story of my adventures as a puppy,
when my best friend, Joe, and his friends were
eight years old and in the third grade.
In this story my pal, Joe, plays a game of basketball
against two big, big boys. This reminds me of the
classic tale **"The Brave Little Tailor."** I imagine
that I am a young tailor who tries to outsmart
two huge, huge giants.
You're in for a real treat, so pull up a chair,
grab a snack, and sink your teeth into
The Brave Little Tailor!

Chapter One

Leashless
in Oakdale

Wishbone trotted away from Beck's Grocery store with his best buddy, Joe Talbot. "'Bye, Ellen!" Wishbone called back to Joe's mom. "Don't forget to buy some puppy-size ginger snaps. And watch out for the guy behind the meat counter. He gets really upset when you put your paws on the glass case."

Ellen went into the store without looking back at the puppy.

Bonk! Bonk! Joe bounced a brown basketball on the sidewalk as he made his way up Oak Street.

"Careful, Joe." Wishbone took two steps away from the basketball. "That's a very *big*

1

ball. I've run into a few balls that size. They can really hurt. One wrong bounce, and you'll have a pancake instead of a Jack Russell terrier puppy."

Wishbone sniffed his way toward the Oakdale post office.

"It's Saturday. It's spring. It's sunny!" he said with glee. He wagged his tail. "And it's a *no-leash* day. What more could a puppy want?"

Something small and orange suddenly danced in front of Wishbone's face.

"A butterfly!" The terrier ran around the side of the building after it.

"Wishbone, come!" Joe called to him.

The little white-with-brown-and-black-spots puppy quickly stopped. He turned and raced back to the sidewalk out front. "Yes, Joe?" He wagged his tail.

"Good boy." Joe scratched Wishbone behind the ears.

Wishbone knew Joe had just made a deal with Ellen. Joe could sometimes let Wishbone off his leash. Joe was trying to teach the puppy to obey commands, even when he was untied. Wishbone was eager to please his pal. And he liked going leashless!

Joe led Wishbone across the street to the schoolyard.

"I just love all this grass!" Wishbone raced back and forth across the lawn in front of the school. Then he caught up with Joe again.

Joe headed around the side of the one-story brick school. He went right to the basketball court. Then he looked at his watch. "I have time to do some practice shots before Sam and David get here." He shook his head. "I really need to work on my game. I haven't been sinking many balls lately."

Sam—short for "Samantha"—and David were Joe and Wishbone's two best friends. They were third-graders, like Joe.

"What you need is a coach, Joe," the puppy said. "Hey, how about me? I have a little experience with balls." Wishbone eyed the basketball in Joe's hand. "They just have not been so big, that's all."

3

Joe dribbled the ball downcourt. He threw it at the hoop. The ball bounced off the rim. It flew right at Wishbone.

"I'm outta here!" Wishbone scrambled to the grass.

Joe caught the ball.

"Take it from me, Joe." Wishbone kept his distance. "A smaller ball would fit through the hoop a lot easier."

Joe took two quick steps back and shot the ball again. This time the ball hit the backboard. It bounced off and went back into Joe's hands. "Oh, no! I missed again."

Joe bounced the ball behind the three-point line.

"Okay, spin and shoot it, Joe!" Wishbone barked.

Turning, Joe leaped up into the air. He threw the ball hard. It dropped through the hoop.

"Did you see that, Wishbone?" Joe ran up and caught the ball when it bounced. He grinned. "I just made a three-point shot!"

"Great!" Wishbone trotted excitedly onto the court. "Uh . . . what's a three-point shot?"

Joe dribbled the ball toward the center of the court again.

"Wait a minute—cute little puppy headed for safety!" Wishbone ran back to the grass.

Suddenly, Joe spun around and raced toward the hoop. He jumped. The ball rolled off his fingertips. It shot up and hit the backboard. Then the ball fell through the net.

"Another two points, Wishbone!" Joe let the ball bounce once. Then he grabbed it. "That's five points in a row!"

"Not bad," said an unfamiliar voice.

Joe and Wishbone turned around.

Wishbone looked up. Two older boys walked onto the court. One of the boys was tall. The other one was even taller, almost a giant. He had a blue-and-red basketball tucked under his arm.

Whoa! Wishbone thought, as he saw the taller boy's shoes. *Look at the size of those sneakers!*

"That was a pretty good layup shot," said the taller boy. "For a little kid."

"Thanks." Joe walked halfway up the court to meet them.

The shorter boy, who really wasn't short at all, bent down. He scratched Wishbone's ears. "Hi, fella. I'm A.J. What's your name?"

Wishbone sniffed A.J.'s hand. Then he licked it. "Wishbone." He tried to lick A.J.'s face, but he couldn't reach it. "You smell and taste okay. You want to play 'chase'?"

"I'm Joe." Joe held his ball tightly. "That's my dog, Wishbone."

Wishbone cocked his head. "Joe, were you listening? I just told him my name."

"Hi." A.J. glanced up at Joe. Then he nodded toward his friend. "That's Stretch."

"Hi," Joe said.

Stretch nodded his head, but he didn't say anything.

Then Joe started to dribble the ball again. He moved downcourt faster and faster. As he got near the basket, he was going full speed.

"Throw it, Joe!" Wishbone called.

Joe jumped and let go of the ball. It sailed into the hoop. Joe looked surprised.

"That's seven points in a row, Joe! I knew you could do it!" Wishbone barked with joy.

"Hey, Stretch, did you see that?" A.J. elbowed his friend. "The kid is good."

Stretch nodded again. "Yeah."

Joe's brown eyes opened wide in surprise. *These big guys think I'm good!* Joe thought.

"*Good?* He's *great!*" Wishbone raced down the court, barking excitedly. "That's seven *in a row!*"

Seven in a row . . . That reminded Wishbone of the story of the brave little tailor. The small tailor knocked out seven thieves—in *one* blow!

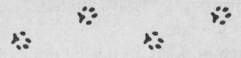

 **Wishbone here! "The Brave Little Tailor" is a fairy tale. It was written down by the Brothers Grimm in the early 1800s. The**

brothers, Jakob and Wilhelm, lived in Germany. They collected stories from around the world. Some of the tales were told to them by friends. Other stories had already been written down on paper by someone else. The Grimm brothers collected more than two hundred stories! These became popular all around the world.

The story of the brave little tailor begins long, long ago. It starts before the tailor had done anything brave. He was just the guy in town who made everyone's clothes. All of the local folks called him the "little tailor." But that was about to change. . . .

Chapter Two

Cool Collar

Wishbone imagined himself as the little tailor. He lived at the edge of town in a small house, and it was a long, long time ago.

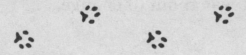

It was a hot day near the end of summer. The little tailor was in his second-favorite room in the house—his sewing room. Rolls of cloth were piled high against one wall. Across the room were open windows. A warm, gentle breeze blew in. Below the windows was a wooden box. It held spools and spools of thread. They were every color of the rainbow. The floor was covered with many different pieces of cloth. They were red, blue, brown, purple, and lots of other bright colors.

The little tailor was at his long wooden table, working. The table sat very low to the ground. It was perfect for somebody of the tailor's size.

The tailor pawed at a coat that had only one sleeve sewn on. "The innkeeper will look perfect in my new fall style. Except for me, he'll have the best coat in town!"

The tailor pinned on the other sleeve. Then he carefully picked up an extra-large needle. With great skill, he stitched the sleeve into place.

"Perfect! Now I think I will take a break." He scratched his neck. "Let me see. Should I have a nap outside on the soft grass? Or should I have a tasty snack?"

The tailor trotted toward the kitchen. *That* was his first-favorite room of the house.

"And the winner is . . . a tasty snack!" He

took out a loaf of bread from the cupboard. The tailor cut two thick slices. He spread a thick layer of blueberry jam on one slice. On the second slice, he spread strawberry jam.

The tailor ate one slice in just a few gulps. Then he took the other piece and trotted back to his sewing room. He set the bread down on his worktable.

"Mm-mmm!" The tailor licked some jam off one of his front paws.

He trotted over and picked up the needle again.

"I'll have these coat sleeves hemmed in no time at all."

As the tailor pushed the needle into the cloth, he saw a fly. It rode in on the breeze coming through the open windows. It buzzed around his bread.

"Shoo!" the tailor barked. "You are as pesky as a flea." But the fly didn't leave. Instead, two more flies joined him. "I'm warning you, you little thieves," the tailor growled. "Get away from my bread and jam!"

12

Suddenly, there were seven big black flies circling over his bread.

"Helllooo! That's *my* snack. Buzz off!"

The flies got closer and closer to the jam.

"Okay, you asked for it, you thieving flies." The little tailor put down his needle. He grabbed a kitchen towel in his mouth. He tried to swat the flies with it. They kept buzzing over his bread. He dropped the towel. Then he leaped onto the table. He landed with his front paws on the slice of bread. His two back

paws landed on the table. The buzzing stopped. The invaders were gone!

The tailor turned his head. He looked from side to side. *Okay, where did they go?* he wondered. *Out the windows?*

He realized his front paws felt squishy. "Hmmm . . ." He lifted his left front paw. Three flies lay dead. The tailor lifted his right front paw. Three more flies lay flattened like buttons! *"Ffth!"* He spat. Another dead fly tumbled from his mouth.

The little tailor took a closer look.

"Seven at a blow! I killed seven with just *one* blow! That's got to be some kind of record. Wait till the guys in town hear this!" He tried to flip in the air to show his excitement. The first time he tried to flip, he landed on his bread. The second time he tried, he stumbled on a thimble. "Maybe flipping on the floor would be a better idea."

He jumped off the table. He licked the jam off his front paws and trotted toward the door of his house. Then he stopped.

14

"I'll stitch the words 'seven in one blow' on my shirt collar. That way everyone in town will know how great I am. Uh . . . did I say *town?*" The little tailor wagged his tail. "This news is too big to stop there. I'll tell the whole countryside. The king, too." The little tailor cocked his head. "I know! I'll offer my services to the king. Why, I'll become his top dog!"

The little tailor gobbled down the rest of his bread. Then he took off his shirt. Using thick black thread, he stitched the words "seven in one blow" onto his collar.

The little tailor put his shirt back on. Then he strapped his sword on his belt. Next, he stepped out into the bright sunshine.

He trotted up the bumpy cobblestone street. All of a sudden he stopped. Out of the corner of his eye, he saw a big white cat. It was getting ready to jump at a bush. Instantly, the little tailor saw why. A small gray bird was hiding in the bush. The bird was so scared he was shaking.

The little tailor went over and gently

picked up the bird. He put him in his shirt pocket. The little tailor turned and stared the cat right in the eye. "Okay, cat! Go pick on something your own size!"

The cat's tail puffed out like a skunk's. He hissed, then turned and ran off.

The little tailor peeked inside his pocket at the bird. "I scared the cat away. You can come out now."

But the bird stayed right where he was. And he didn't make a peep.

"Did the cat get your tongue?" asked the tailor. "It's a joke. Get it?" Not a sound from the bird. The little tailor laughed as he trotted on. "You can stay in my pocket if you want," the tailor said.

The bird gave one little chirp.

The little tailor made his way to the center of town. It was market day. Heavy wooden carts filled the street. They were piled high with carrots, cabbages, and potatoes. Up and down the street, people were busy buying and trading goods.

"I just killed seven thieves in one blow!" the tailor called out proudly. "Pretty neat, huh?"

The shoppers stared at the tailor. Then they whispered to one another.

But with his super-sensitive ears, the tailor could hear every word.

"Seven in one blow . . . the little tailor has killed seven in one blow!"

The tailor held his head high as he trotted along. *Nobody has to know it was seven* flies. *Right?*

When the little tailor had walked far away

from the town, he stopped. He sniffed the air. In front of him was a mountain. The little tailor started to climb up a steep dirt path. "Yup. This looks like the way to the king's palace." Pine trees lined both sides of the path. The higher the tailor went, the bigger the trees grew. And the steeper the path got. "Whew!" The little tailor panted. His tongue hung out of his mouth.

The bird in his pocket didn't make a chirp. But he was beginning to wiggle around in his new "nest."

"Hey, that tickles," the little tailor said. Suddenly, the ground beneath his paws shook. Then it shook again. The tailor heard a thud. He froze in his tracks. He perked up his ears and listened. He heard another thud! *Someone is walking close by,* he thought. *Someone with very big feet!*

At that moment, a big dark shadow fell over him. The tailor looked up . . . then up some more.

"Uh-oh."

In front of the little tailor stood a man the size of a whale. The frightening figure frowned. The tailor frowned. *It's one of those fee-fi-fo-fum guys! Suddenly, I feel like a four-legged ant—way too small!*

Wishbone here! The tailor may be in trouble. In the meantime, let's see how Joe is getting along on the basketball court.

Chapter Three

The Challenge

Stretch walked up to Joe. He looked back at A.J. Then he looked at Joe. "Hey, kid, do you think you would be interested in playing a three-way game?"

"You mean every man for himself?" Joe tucked the basketball under his arm.

Stretch nodded. "Right. You, me, and A.J. We'll each be a one-man team. First guy to get ten points wins."

Joe stood there, thinking.

"Go for it, Joe." Wishbone wagged his tail at Joe.

"Well?" Stretch held his basketball up in the air.

"Sure." Joe grinned. He walked off the court. He set his ball down on the grass.

Wishbone trotted up behind him.

"Stay, Wishbone." Joe walked onto the court again.

"Got it, Joe." Wishbone sat down. "My training is going well. Don't you think so?" He stared at Joe's brown basketball. "Not so tough now, are you?" he said to the ball. "On the ground you're about as dangerous as a day-old kitten."

"We all use the same basket." A.J. nodded to the one behind Stretch. He walked toward the basket.

Joe followed him. "Right."

Stretch spun the ball on the tip of his first finger. He grinned down at Joe. "With three people playing, you usually don't have a tip-off. But I thought you could use the practice, kid." Stretch kept spinning the ball. "You can toss up the ball for A.J. and me. You're so small, you wouldn't have a chance against either one of us."

"Okay," Joe agreed.

Wishbone moved to the edge of the court. "That sounds good, Joe!" He wagged his tail. "Uh . . . what's a tip-off? I need to learn these basketball words."

Stretch handed his ball to Joe. Then he and A.J. high-fived each other.

Joe stepped between them. "Ready?"

"Ready," the two older boys said.

Joe tossed the ball high into the air. The two big boys jumped up. Joe moved back out of their way.

Stretch and A.J. each reached for the ball. Stretch's long fingers slapped it. It flew toward Joe.

"Jump for it, Joe!" Wishbone said.

Joe put his hands up high. But the ball sailed over his head. Joe turned to chase it.

In one giant step, Stretch was beside Joe. A.J. was on the other side of Joe.

Wow! These guys are really fast! Wishbone thought.

Another big step, and Stretch snatched

the ball from the air. A.J. was right in front of him.

Stretch dribbled the ball around A.J.

Wishbone was getting dizzy. *Stretch leans one way, and A.J. does the same. Stretch sticks an arm up, and so does A.J. Weird . . . This double stuff is making me seasick! Oh . . . oh . . .* Wishbone's stomach began to roll back and forth. He shook himself to get rid of the feeling. Then he looked at Joe. Joe was following the bigger boys around like a lost puppy.

"Hey, I know what they are doing!" Wishbone stood up. He ran to the end of the court.

Stretch shot. He made a basket. Joe rushed over to get the ball. A.J. beat him to it.

"They're doing the double stuff again, Joe." Wishbone looked down at their big feet. "Remember when that huge dog stole my chew toy? Do what I did—just go between the legs. Then grab the ball and run."

A.J. shot and missed. Stretch jumped high and grabbed the loose ball. He tried to shoot in midair, but he lost his balance.

Suddenly, Joe stuck his hand in between the two big boys' ankles. He slapped the ball back toward himself. The ball went through Stretch's legs. With his other hand, Joe then grabbed the ball.

The big boys were so surprised that they stopped moving.

Finally, Stretch leaped sideways. But one big foot tripped the other one. Stretch lost his balance again. He placed a hand down on the court to keep from falling.

Joe shot. The ball hit the backboard, then dropped through the hoop. He went for the rebound. Joe got the ball and took another shot. The ball sank through the net again.

"Another basket for my buddy! Four points!" Wishbone jumped excitedly. "Am I good at coaching, or what?"

Joe went for the blue-and-red ball again.

"Time!" Stretch called.

Joe turned before he could get the ball. It bounced toward Stretch.

Joe and A.J. looked at Stretch.

"What's up?" A.J. asked.

Wishbone ran over to Joe. "I think he means snack time."

Stretch picked up the ball. "I want to go one-on-one with the little hotshot." He nodded at Joe. "Let's see what you can really do."

Then there was nothing but silence. All eyes were on Joe.

Wishbone here! Will Joe take the Stretch challenge? The pressure is on. . . .

In the meantime, let's see what's happening with the little tailor, who is starting to feel some pressure of his own.

Chapter Four

Helping the Giant

"**H**ellloooo, up there!" the little tailor called up to the giant. His heart pounded in his chest. *This guy is as tall as the pine trees. He could pick up and eat a whole* cart *of cabbages in one bite. And look at the size of his arms. They're as thick as tree trunks. I wonder what vitamins he takes!*

The giant leaned down toward the tailor. His long, tangled hair fell forward. The tailor noticed that the giant's clothes were covered in dirt. So were his bare feet and hands. *I'm all for skipping one or two baths. But this guy smells worse than a family of skunks!*

"What are you doing on *my* mountain?" The giant's voice boomed and echoed.

The little tailor stepped back. "Uh . . . this is your mountain?"

The giant frowned.

"Uh . . . well, I'm just passing through." The tailor wagged his tail nervously. "I'm on my way to the palace—to help the king!"

The giant squinted one huge eye at him. "How can someone so small help the king?"

The little tailor sat down. He tipped his head to the side. "Look at my shirt collar." *Hmm . . .* he wondered. *Maybe giants can't read.* Then he had another thought. *Or maybe they like tailors as between-meal snacks!* The tailor jumped to his feet quickly. "My collar says 'seven in one blow.' You know why?" The tailor didn't give the giant time to answer. "Oh, this is so cool." He jumped around excitedly. "Because I killed seven thieves in *one* blow."

"Is that so?" The giant stood up straight. He rubbed his big grizzly chin with one hand. Then he reached down and picked up a huge rock. It was the size of a watermelon! "Watch this," he said.

The little tailor looked at the giant. He threw the rock above his head. It sailed higher and higher into the air. Finally, it was so far up it looked like a flea. Then the rock flew back to the ground. *Thunk!* The earth shook.

"Good arm," said the little tailor.

The giant crossed his thick arms over his wide chest. "Let's see you match that!"

"Okay." *Let me see. . . . In just a few seconds I have to think of a way to out-throw a giant!*

The little tailor thought. All of a sudden, he squirmed sideways and laughed. The bird in his pocket was tickling him again. *That's it!* he thought.

"Let me find just the right rock," the little tailor told the giant. "Then I will show you something even better." He turned his tail to the giant. Bending over, the tailor pretended to look for a rock. He gently took the bird from his pocket. The tailor hid it in his paws. "To the moon," he whispered to the bird.

Then the tailor faced the giant again.

"Okay, now watch this," he said. The little

29

tailor tossed the bird high up into the air. The bird looked just like a gray rock.

It flew up and up and up. Finally, the bird disappeared high in the blue sky.

All right! The little tailor jumped excitedly. "Satisfied? Now, if you don't mind, I'll be on my way."

"Humpf!" The giant frowned. He put out a huge hand to block the tailor.

The little tailor stopped short. "I will take that as a 'no.'"

The giant rubbed his chin again. He pointed at a big oak tree that had fallen on the ground. "If you are so strong, let's see you help me carry that tree back to my den."

The tailor trotted over and pawed the thickest part of the tree trunk. "You can carry this end right here," the tailor said. Then he moved to the other end of the tree. "I'll carry all these branches at the top."

"It's a deal!" the giant said happily, thinking he had made out the best.

The little tailor walked under his end of

the tree. It looked as if the branches were resting on his shoulder.

The giant grabbed the thick tree trunk. Grunting, he lifted it onto his shoulder.

I can't see him, thought the little tailor. *And he can't see me. Perfect.* "Lead the way!" he hollered to the giant.

The tree began to move forward. The giant was going up the mountain. The little tailor quickly jumped up onto a branch. He found a good spot and sat down. The giant was carrying the tree and the tailor!

Soon the giant stopped. Grunting, he started to lift the tree off his shoulder.

The little tailor jumped down. He pretended he was carrying his end of the tree.

The giant set the tree on the ground. He wiped his sweaty face with his arm. "You must be tired," the giant said to the tailor. The earth shook as the giant sat down. He leaned against a leafy tree.

The little tailor raced circles around the giant. "No, I'm not tired at all."

The giant frowned. He let out a long, low growl.

The brave little tailor turned and raced away. When he was safely out of the giant's reach, the tailor sat and looked back at him. *I see* somebody *gets a little cranky when he's tired.*

Chapter Five

Double Trouble

After the giant rested, he stood up. He glared down at the little tailor. "Let's go. My den isn't much farther from here."

With your long legs and big feet, nothing *must be too far away!* the tailor thought. He raced to his end of the tree. Again he stood so that it looked as if the branches rested on his shoulder.

The giant bent over and grabbed the huge tree trunk. With a loud groan, he lifted it up.

"Ready at this end!" yelled the tailor. All he could see in front of him were leaves and branches. But he could *smell* the giant.

Then the tree began to move forward. The

tailor quickly jumped up onto a branch. The giant climbed higher and higher onto the mountain. Finally, he came to a stop. He set his end on the ground.

We must be at his den—whatever that is.

The tailor jumped down from his branch. He glanced around. He was at the very top of the mountain. It would be dark soon. And there he was, all alone with some huge, smelly guy!

The giant was huffing and puffing. He looked very tired. "Follow me!" he ordered. He led the tailor to a huge rock wall that was hidden by trees. There was an opening in the wall. It was high and rounded at the top. The open space led inside a dark cave. The giant motioned for the little tailor to go in.

The little tailor sniffed at the entrance. "Mmm . . . I smell food." He wagged his tail. "I'm in a bit of a hurry. Could I get my meal to go? Then if you could just point me in the—"

The giant roared.

The tailor jumped inside the cave. "On

second thought, maybe I will come in. Just for a minute."

The path was a tunnel. Inside was cold and dark. Up ahead, he could see firelight. It flickered against the wall of the path. The brave little tailor heard a crunching noise.

Finally, he walked through the tunnel and into a room. It was a very, very big room. At one end was a fireplace. A second giant sat on a tree stump near the fire. He had long, stringy hair. Chunks of dried-up food were stuck in his beard. They looked like flies trapped in a spiderweb. His shirt was so small that it didn't even cover his belly. In one hand the giant held a meaty, greasy drumstick. He ripped a big bite from it with his sharp teeth.

That's no drumstick, the little tailor thought. *It only looks like a drumstick because the giant is holding it in his hand. It's a* whole *roasted lamb!*

The little tailor looked around. The "den" was just a rock cave. The ground was gray. The ceiling was gray. And the walls were gray.

There were two tree stumps. The giants used them as chairs. A third stump had an axe stuck in it. The little tailor shivered. *I hope that's only for chopping firewood.*

The tailor noticed that the smelly giant was eyeing him. It was a frightening stare. The tailor looked at the giant who was eating. He was eyeing the tailor, too.

Guys, did anyone ever tell you it's not polite to stare? The tailor scratched his neck nervously.

The giant holding the food crunched down on a bone. Gnawing on it, he leaned toward the tailor. Then he pointed a greasy, fat finger at the words on the tailor's collar. "What does that mean?" the giant said with a grunt. The tailor noticed that his teeth were the color of spinach.

The tailor stepped back. "It means I killed seven thieves with just one blow!"

"Oh?" The giant sounded amazed.

"That's right." The tailor stepped back even more. He wanted to try to stay out of the giant's reach. "And now I am on my way to offer my services to the king. So if you will just tell me—"

"The king?" repeated the bone-cruncher. "You are going to help the king?"

"That's right." The little tailor watched the giants trade puzzled looks. "Uh . . . is there a problem?"

Both giants quickly shook their big, heavy heads. "No, no, not at all," they both said.

"By now it's dark outside," the bone-cruncher said slyly. "You had better sleep here tonight. You never know what you might run

into after dark in those cold woods." He finished tearing off the last bits of meat from the bone. Then he licked his fingers with loud slurping noises. "The mountain is filled with all kinds of strange, creepy critters."

Yeah, I know. And I'm looking at two of them right here, thought the little tailor. He started backing out very slowly toward the entrance of the cave door.

A roar rumbled through the den.

The tailor jumped forward.

"We insist that you stay here." The smelly giant grabbed the tailor by his collar. "Come with me!"

"Uh . . . well . . . okay. Since you put it that way—"

The giant dragged the tailor down another tunnel. Only the glow from the fire behind them lit their way. Soon they reached another room. In one corner was a low wooden bed. It had a bare mattress on it. The rest of the room was empty.

The giant threw the little tailor inside.

"Uh . . . would you have something a little cozier?" The tailor looked back at the giant in the dim light. The giant was grinning. The fur on the tailor's neck bristled.

The giant turned and stomped off, leaving the tailor all alone.

"I'll take that as a 'no,'" the tailor called. "You could at least say 'sleep tight and don't let the bedbugs bite.'" The tailor shook off a shiver. Then, grabbing the end of his belt, he removed his sword. "The more I think about it, bedbugs are not my biggest problem in this place."

The little tailor laid his sword by the foot of the bed. Then he jumped up onto the mattress. It was stuffed with straw. He circled three times, then dropped to his belly. A sharp piece of straw stuck out of the dirty, damp mattress. It poked his stomach. He rolled onto his side to move away from it. Another piece of straw poked him right in the ear. He pawed it. The straw still poked his ear.

With a growl, the little tailor moved to the

other end of the mattress. He lay down. More straw poked him through another tear in the mattress. He scratched his side. It wouldn't stop itching. *What if it's* not *the straw? What if there really are bedbugs in here? They're worse than fleas!*

The little tailor jumped down from the mattress. "I think a spot in the corner will do just fine." He curled up on the cold, hard-rock ground. He stopped itching. He closed his eyes. "First thing tomorrow morning, I'm outta here!"

The tailor fell asleep. He dreamed about

the nice soft bed that he would have when he reached the king's palace.

It was pitch-dark when the tailor half-opened his eyes. His ears twitched to pick up sounds. *Sounds like . . . great big . . . sneaky footsteps. Giants' footsteps!*

The tailor opened his eyes wide. Without moving, he stared across the dark room. He could not see a thing. But he didn't have to. He sniffed. *Both fee-fi-fo-fum fellows are in here with me. Uh-oh . . .*

Finally, the little tailor could see a shape. One giant stood near the bed. He had his hands raised high over his head. He was holding some kind of a big club. A log! *Okay, the good thing about this is . . . Well, I guess there is no good thing about this! Yikes!*

Wishbone here! It looks as if the giants are up to no good.

Meanwhile, let's head on back to Oakdale to see how Joe is handling the giant boys on the basketball court.

Chapter Six

Add Up Points

Joe stared wide-eyed at Stretch.

"What's it going to be?" Stretch stood with his feet apart. They were firmly planted on the basketball court. "Will you go one-on-one with me or not?"

Joe was nervous. He looked up into Stretch's eyes. "You're on."

"That's my boy!" the puppy said happily. "Size is not everything. I'll show you. See what I can do?" He jumped and ran around. Turning, he bumped into Joe's brown basketball, laying in the grass. It wobbled, rolled, then stopped.

"Stay!" Wishbone charged away from the

big ball. He plopped down at the edge of the basketball court. "Okay. I'm ready now. You can start playing."

A.J. walked off the court. "I'm the ref," he called.

"Fine. First one to get six points wins." Stretch tossed the ball hard to Joe. "We are playing two points per basket."

The force of the throw pushed Joe back. He took a deep breath. He looked at Stretch and nodded.

"Time in!" A.J. started the game.

Joe spun around. His back faced Stretch. He dribbled the ball away.

In one leap Stretch was beside Joe.

Joe looked surprised.

Stretch reached out easily and stole the ball. He shot and made the basket.

Joe looked even more surprised.

"Way to go!" A.J. called to his friend. "Two points for Stretch."

Stretch bounced the ball over to Joe. He grinned. "You're behind."

"The game's just starting." Joe held the red-and-blue ball with both hands.

"Yeah." The puppy ran alongside the court to cheer on his pal. "Don't worry, Joe. You'll catch up."

When A.J. called time in, Joe dribbled the ball into play.

Wishbone was too excited to stand still. "Shoot, Joe. Shoot it now!"

Joe tried to aim for the basket. But Stretch was right in front of him.

For a second Joe froze—as if he could not decide what to do next.

Stretch knocked the ball out of Joe's hands. In one smooth move, Stretch passed the ball behind his back. He caught the ball with his other hand. Leaping up in the air, Stretch took careful aim and then shot and made another basket.

"Four points." Stretch grinned as he ran to catch the ball.

Joe sighed and glanced at Wishbone. There was a worried look on his face.

"Hey, big guy!" Wishbone barked at Stretch. "Don't be a big ball hog."

A.J. waited until Stretch passed the ball to Joe. "Time in," he called again.

Dribbling the ball, Joe turned right. But Stretch was right there beside him. Joe leaned to the left. He tried to shoot. Stretch tried to block Joe's shot. Stretch's elbow hit Joe's arm.

"Time!" A.J. yelled. He stopped the game. "A foul on Stretch. Joe gets two foul shots."

"All right!" Joe dribbled the ball back behind the white foul line. He stared at the hoop.

"Oh, come on! I didn't foul!" Stretch folded his long arms across his chest.

"Hurry up and shoot, buddy," Wishbone said. "Just get those points!"

Joe bounced the ball once. He raised his arms up. Then he released the ball from his fingertips. It soared high through the air. But it missed the hoop completely.

"Oh!" Wishbone quickly covered one eye with a paw.

Joe frowned. "I can't believe the ball didn't even touch the backboard."

Stretch tossed the ball over to Joe again. "Believe it, kid."

"Tough break, buddy." Wishbone walked back and forth along the sideline. As the puppy made a turn, he bumped into Joe's big brown basketball. "Sorry." With his muzzle, he pushed the ball away.

The ball kept rolling. It didn't stop.

"Joe!" the puppy called. The ball was headed toward a grassy hill. Wishbone looked back at his pal. "Joe! Joe!" he barked.

But Joe was getting ready to take another foul shot.

Wishbone sighed. He glanced back at Joe's brown ball. It was still rolling. It was nearing the edge of the hill.

"Joe!" the puppy called out again. He ran toward the hill. "Could I get some help over here?"

Wishbone looked down and saw the ball. It was headed toward the thorn bushes in a ditch.

"Helllooo!" Wishbone called to the kids.

But no one turned to look at him.

Wishbone sighed. "I can't wait until I'm full-grown. Then they'll listen to me!"

He watched the brown ball as it picked up more and more speed.

"I have a big problem on my paws. . . ."

"Here goes." Joe shot the ball into the air. It hit the edge of the backboard. It bounced off and fell to the ground.

Joe shook his head and sighed.

"Boy, I have a problem. My foul shots are

not even coming close to the basket. I need a lot of shooting practice. I'll keep practicing until I'm the best there is."

Wishbone looked back and forth from the hill to Joe. "Okay, Joe. I guess we both have a problem. But mine really, really, *really* needs attention now!"

Wishbone here! Joe is in big trouble. The score is 4–0, and Joe's slump has not ended. *And* the brown basketball is getting away! Let's trot on over and catch up with the little tailor. We'll see how he is doing with his double trouble—the giants.

Chapter Seven

Surrounded

Wham! One of the giants slammed a log down on the mattress. *Wham! Wham!* He did it again . . . and again.

The tailor lay still in the corner of the room. His heart pounded heavily in his furred chest. Suddenly, he got an itch behind his ear. *Can't move. They'll hear me. Can't move . . . can't move!* he warned himself in the darkness.

The giant let out a grunt that echoed throughout the cave. *Wham! Wham! Wham!* The wooden bed crumbled to splinters. Bits of straw from the mattress flew into the air.

"That's the end of that little pest," said the giant holding the log.

"You squashed him like a flea," said the other giant. "Killing his chance of ever becoming a royal pain in the neck."

The giants let out big belly laughs. They stomped out of the dark room.

They compared me to a flea. The little tailor scratched his ear. *The nerve of them!* He laid his head down on his paws. He closed his eyes, but he could not go to sleep. *What if the giants come back for me?* wondered the tailor. Then he remembered that the giants thought he was dead. The den was so quiet that he was sure the giants had gone to sleep.

Finally, the little tailor himself fell asleep.

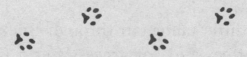

Early the next morning, the little tailor heard the giants leave the den. Their rumbling footsteps slowly faded away into the distance. He stretched. He belted on his sword. Then, in the dim light, he trotted back to the room where the fire was. A big chunk of roasted lamb lay on the tree stump. The tailor wagged his tail with glee.

"Now, this is some meal!" He chewed hungrily on the hunk of roasted meat. "Mm-mmm. Breakfast—one of my favorite meals."

When he was full, the little tailor sniffed his way out of the den. He looked around in the early-morning light. Two dirt paths led down the mountain in the direction he was going.

"Eenie, meanie, minie, moe . . ." The tailor sniffed one path, then the other. "Only my nose knows which way to go." He started down the path that was on the same side as his spotted ear. "I guess the king's palace is this way!"

The little tailor ran through thick groups of pine trees and oak trees. After a while he turned a corner. An awful smell filled the air. There, in front of him, stood the giants! Their backs were to him.

Oh, no. Not again. The little tailor quietly started to back away. But he accidentally stepped on a twig. The giants heard him.

The huge creatures twisted around. Their faces went pale and their mouths fell open.

"You're not dead!" croaked the giant that the tailor had nicknamed "bone-cruncher." He stepped back from the tailor. Both giants looked . . . scared.

Why, they're afraid of me! thought the tailor. "Hmm . . . let me see." The tailor walked forward. "Heart's beating, legs are moving, and I'm talking." He wagged his tail at the giants. "Nope. I'm not dead."

"He's come to kill us!" yelled the smelly giant in a rumbling voice. "Run!"

The giants turned in different directions. They thundered off through the trees.

"See you around, fellas!" The little tailor barked after them. Soon the giants were out of sight. The tailor whistled and trotted along on his way to meet the king. He followed his nose down the mountain.

He saw fewer and fewer trees. The tailor looked across the valley that lay ahead of him. Not too far away was a huge palace. It was long and rose high above the fields. A rock wall went all the way around it.

"That must be the king's place!" The little tailor's sharp eyesight helped him see tiny shops and houses just outside the wall.

The little tailor hurried on. Panting, he finally reached the wall. Spaced out along the top of the wall were huge heads carved from stone. Every head was exactly the same—a snarling catlike creature. Each one had big pointed teeth.

"Cats . . . Some people have no taste."

The tailor sprang up on his back paws. He tried to jump over the wall. He sprang again and again. But he didn't even come close to getting over.

"Okay, moving on . . ." He put his nose to the bottom of the rock wall. The tailor quickly sniffed his way along. He was looking for the best place to dig.

Suddenly, the tailor stopped what he was doing and looked up.

"A gate! And the iron bars are so far apart that two of me could fit through them at one time!"

The tailor leaped between the bars. He was inside the palace courtyard.

"Wow!"

The grass there was the greenest he had ever seen! He rolled joyfully in it.

After a while he got up and walked over to a big maple tree. "I'll just lie down in the shade and rest. Then I will go meet the king." He dropped down to the ground. The grass felt cool on his belly. "Ah . . ." A minute later the little tailor was sound asleep.

"Seven in one blow!" a voice whispered.

"Seven!" another repeated.

The words broke into the little tailor's sleep. He opened his eyes. Looking up, he saw a circle of soldiers staring down at him. *Oh, I just* love *being the center of attention!*

One soldier touched the words stitched on the tailor's collar. "You must be very brave to fight seven at once."

"Brave—that's me." The little tailor jumped to his paws. "I am a tailor, and I killed seven thieves with one blow!" He flipped in the air.

Frightened, the soldiers jumped back.

The tailor wagged his tail. "Don't worry. I'm here to see the king. I'm sure that he will love having a brave guy like me around. I could come in handy."

The soldiers looked at one another. They whispered back and forth.

The brave little tailor perked up his ears. With his super hearing, he could hear the men. They were agreeing with one another. They thought the tailor would be good to have around. He could save their necks in a battle with the enemy!

Finally, the soldier in charge smiled. "Come. I will take you to meet the king."

The soldier walked the tailor to the palace door. The door was high, with a big arch at the top—like a giant horseshoe. The huge wooden door was painted white, with gold trim. A heavy gold ring for knocking hung on the door.

Lifting the knocker, the soldier banged it against the door three times. The door swung open. A servant listened while the soldier explained his mission. With a nod, he moved aside and let them in.

"Thank you." The little tailor stepped into a big hallway. The cool marble floor felt good on his paws. He eyed the dark walls. High up along both sides hung paintings of kings. Each was in a gold frame.

Just ahead of the tailor was a staircase that was covered in dark red carpet. Railing posts held thick candles to light the way.

Suddenly, a young lady came running down the stairs. She wore a flowing pink-satin dress. Her long yellow hair was pulled back. It was tied with a pink ribbon.

The little tailor sighed. "Isn't she just the cutest thing you ever saw!"

"Have more respect, tailor. That's the king's daughter—the princess," the soldier said. "Bow!"

"I'll say! Bow . . . *wow!*" The tailor bowed down, along with the soldier.

The princess did not pay any attention to the tailor. When she was gone, the soldier hurried down a hallway. "Follow me."

They walked past high arched doorways. Each led to a room that had the most beautiful wooden furniture the little tailor had ever

seen. *I wonder what kind of trouble I would get into for chewing on one of those table legs,* he thought.

Finally, they entered a room that had a guard posted at the doorway. The tailor spotted the king. He was sitting on a big red throne-chair. His robe was royal blue. His dark, wavy hair hung down just below his ears. On top of his head was a gold crown. It sparkled with red jewels the size of gumdrops.

"What is it?" The king scratched at the neatly trimmed beard on his chin.

The soldier took one stiff step forward and bowed. "This man is very brave. He would like to serve you, Your Highness."

The little tailor trotted forward. Then he bowed down on his front paws. Standing again, he stuck out his chest. "I killed seven thieves in one blow. So I thought you could use a brave guy like me around the palace."

"Oh?" The king eyed him. Then, squinting, he shook a ringed finger in the air. "You have a point. And I have just the job for you."

"I just knew it!" The tailor wagged his tail full speed.

Bending down, the king looked the little tailor right in the eye. "We have two terrible neighbors. They come in the night to rob and kill my people. We have not been able to stop them." Then the king stood up. "If you can stop them, I will give you half my kingdom. And I will let you marry my only daughter."

The little tailor flipped. *Whoo-hoo! My own kingdom . . . and the princess! All I have to do is get rid of a couple of bad guys.* "It's a deal! Now, exactly where do these nasty neighbors live?"

The king grinned slyly. "The giants? Oh, they live in the woods that are high up on the mountain."

The little tailor scratched his neck with a back paw. "Uh . . . are you talking about two really big, big guys? Who live in a cave? One is smelly, and the other looks as if he uses his beard for a napkin?"

"Yes, that would be them," said the king. "Are they friends of yours?"

A picture of the bed-smashing giant flashed into the tailor's mind. A shiver ran down his furred spine. "Well, they did try to smash me to bits. So I would not call them friends."

Chapter Eight

Double Trouble Again

The little tailor turned and began to trot out of the king's throne room.

"Wait!" called the king. "I will send one hundred of my best soldiers with you."

"Thank you." *What a nice guy,* the tailor thought as he left.

Trotting out of the palace, the tailor saw the princess in the courtyard. She was there planting purple and white flowers.

"Helllooo!" called the tailor.

"Oh, hi, there!" The princess smiled and waved to him.

The tailor wagged his tail excitedly. He wished he could run over and kiss the fair lady's hand. *I like to* dig *holes. She likes to* plant *flowers. Wow! We're perfect for each other!*

All of a sudden, soldiers rode up on horses. They were brave-looking men. They wore silver helmets on their heads. And their bodies were covered in steel armor. The leader was the one who had taken the little tailor to see the king.

The brave little tailor jumped through the open gate of the palace. He pointed his black nose at the mountain. "Follow me, men!" He raced away. Then he glanced back at all the horses. Their hooves were pounding the dirt. The dirt scattered in all directions. The tailor pumped his four legs even harder. "Just don't get *too* close!"

The tailor and the soldiers made their way up the steep mountainside.

Before long they neared the top. *How am I going to get rid of the two giants?* The brave little tailor had to decide quickly.

"Whoa!" He turned and called out to the soldiers. "You guys wait here while I go into the woods. The horses are noisy. If the giants hear them, they will hide."

The head soldier looked relieved. "But don't you want our help?"

"Nope. Remember, I killed seven with one blow. These two will not be a problem." *At least I hope not,* he thought. The little tailor put his skilled nose to the ground. He sniffed his way along. As he got closer to the giants' den, he heard a great rumbling. The ground trembled. He heard another rumbling and the ground trembled again. The tailor dropped to his belly. Quietly, he crawled through the trees, toward the noise. The branches of an oak tree in the distance were shaking. The tailor made his way carefully. Looking under the tree, the tailor spotted both of the giants.

Perfect. The tailor wagged his tail. *They're sleeping like babies! Well . . . make that babies with very bad snoring problems.*

Staying hidden, the tailor watched the giants closely and tried to think up a plan. He remembered the rock-tossing contest he had had with the first giant. *I think I've got it!*

The little tailor scooped up rocks. He dropped them into his shirt pockets. *Ready or not, guys, here I come!* He looked around to find a way to get up into the oak tree that hung over the giants.

The tailor saw a tall, thin tree that leaned to one side. It was almost touching the big oak tree that hung over the giants' heads.

The little tailor climbed up the thin tree. When he saw a thick branch just above the giants, he jumped for it. The branch swayed as he landed on it. It threw him off balance for a moment. *So . . . this is what it feels like to be a squirrel!* he thought. *I prefer my four-on-the-floor any day!*

Quickly, he took out the smallest rocks he had collected. Leaning over, the little tailor dropped the rocks one at a time onto the dirty, smelly giant.

Plink! Plink! Plink! The rocks bounced off the creature's big, round belly.

The giant woke up with a frown. He pushed the other giant. "Why are you hitting me?"

"You are dreaming," said the bone-cruncher. "I didn't touch you." He rolled over so that his back faced the other giant.

Grumbling, the smelly giant closed his eyes.

The little tailor wagged his tail. *Am I good, or what?* He waited in silence. When the giants went back to sleep, the tailor dug a bigger rock out of his pocket. He took aim. Then he dropped it right onto the middle of the smelly giant's bulging chest.

"This is too much!" The giant jumped up. He hit the other giant so hard that he fell against the tree trunk. The tree swayed back and forth.

The little tailor hung on tightly to keep from crashing to the ground. *Guys—you are getting a little too close!*

"Leave me alone!" said the bone-cruncher. He ripped a full-grown tree out of the ground.

Swinging it like a club, he whacked the other giant on the neck.

The brave little tailor wagged his tail. *One blow from each giant. That makes it a tie game—one to one!*

"Hey!" The smelly giant reached over and yanked another tree out of the ground. He slammed the other giant over the head. "*You* leave *me* alone!"

The bone-cruncher swayed. "You asked for it!" He bonked his buddy over the head.

"You are nothing but a big cry-baby and a grump!" His friend returned the blow.

The two giants kept beating each other. In the end, both giants crashed to the ground and lay still. The tailor could see they were dead. Beside them were their clubs.

The brave little tailor carefully made his way down the thin tree trunk. He trotted over to the giants. He wagged his tail. "Good job, guys. So nice of you to do each other in!"

Behind him, he heard hoofbeats. *Uh-oh. The king's soldiers are coming!*

71

The tailor pulled the sword out from his sheath. He looked at the giants. "Sorry, fellas. But you will not feel a thing—honest."

With the tip of his sword, the tailor poked one giant in the shoulder. Then he poked the other giant in his big, puffy chest. Just as he put his sword away, the band of soldiers rode up.

A few soldiers jumped down from their horses. The leader saw the fallen giants. "You killed them!" He sounded surprised. "Are you hurt?"

"They pulled up trees to defend themselves," said the little tailor. "But they did not harm a hair on my head." He wagged his tail. "Or anywhere else, for that matter."

The soldier turned and shouted to the other men. "He has killed the giants. And he is unharmed!"

The soldiers crowded in for a better look. "Oh!" They let out a gasp when they saw the bloody giants.

"You are truly a very brave man," said

the leader of the group. "You will make a fine addition to the king's service."

"Yes," said another. "We would not even dare to fight *one* of the giants. You fought them both at once. And you won!"

The little tailor scratched his side. "Cool, huh! Well . . . all in a day's work. Now, let's go and tell the king."

"You must be tired from all that fighting. You can ride my horse back to the palace." One of the soldiers helped the tailor up onto his horse. They rode back down the mountain. Just before dark, they reached the palace.

"Thanks for the ride." The little tailor slid back-paws-first off the horse.

The tailor hurried inside the palace. He trotted from room to room.

"Hello! Mr. King, where are you?" the tailor called, his voice echoing off the stone walls.

The tailor put his nose in the air and sniffed.

"Is that turkey potpie I smell?" He ran past a servant and headed toward the large dining hall. "Excuse me! Brave guy coming through." He trotted past the guard at the doorway.

A long table was in the center of the room. It was covered with a clean white cloth. At one end of the table sat the princess. She was picking at a piece of pie. Seeing the tailor, she smiled and wiggled her fingers in the air at him.

Oh! Look at all that dirt under her nails. The brave little tailor wagged his tail. *A woman who understands dirt. This is just so great!*

Finally, he looked to the other end of the table. The king was there, eating a pie right out of the pie pan.

"Great news," said the tailor. "Both of the giants are dead." He walked over and put a paw on the king's robe. "Now, how about some of that pie? Oh, and you can also give me my half of the kingdom."

"Well, well—you killed both giants!" The king wiped his food-splattered face on the white tablecloth. "Very good. You must be tired and want to rest. We'll talk more about this kingdom deal in the morning." He clapped his hands twice.

Four armed soldiers hurried through the doorway.

"Show this man to our *guest* room!" he boomed.

The soldiers quickly formed a circle around the little tailor.

"But I'm not tired," said the tailor. He took a suspicious step backward. "Really."

But the soldiers had him surrounded like a human cage. Then they marched him out of the dining hall.

Chapter Nine

A Surprise for the King

"**O**kay, maybe going to my room isn't such a bad idea. I am a little tired now that I think of it," said the tailor as the soldiers walked him down a hall. It was lit by thick candles hanging in holders on the walls.

The soldiers looked straight ahead. They did not speak. All of a sudden they stopped. One of them opened a heavy, creaking door. The soldiers pushed the tailor into the nearly dark room.

"Hey! That's no way to say good-night."

The tailor landed in a pile of scratchy straw. Then the door slammed shut behind him. He heard a key turn in a lock.

Starlight shone through a tiny window in one wall. The little tailor peered around the room. There was nothing in it but the straw he had landed on. "Even the big, mean giants gave me a better guest room than this." *It's more like a jail cell or a dungeon than a guest room.* He sniffed along the cold stone floor. *Maybe the last guest left a few crumbs. . . . Nope. I wonder if they have room service here.*

The tailor's head popped up. He perked up his ears. There were footsteps and voices just outside his door.

He heard more footsteps. This time they were going *away* from his room. Then his door slowly opened. "Princess!" The little tailor wagged his tail.

After slipping into the room, the princess shut the door carefully. She pulled something from her lace shawl.

"I brought you pie and water," she said. She kneeled down beside him. "And also a warning," she whispered.

"What kind of warning?" The little tailor

sniffed the turkey potpie. *Yum!* He locked his teeth around a thick piece of tender meat.

"I heard my father order the guards to grab you in your sleep."

"Wow! I get it." The tailor licked gravy from his lips. "The king has another job for me. Does he want me to kill more giants?"

"No." The princess shook her head. "My father and his soldiers are afraid of you. My father will never give you half his kingdom. He will not let you marry me, either." She glanced over at the door. "The soldiers plan to kidnap you while you sleep. Then they will carry you away on a ship."

The tailor was beginning to catch on to the plan. "Uh . . . let me guess. I will not be traveling first class?"

The princess lowered her head. "My father ordered his soldiers to kill you at sea. Then they will dump you overboard."

"But I am one of the good guys! I only came to the palace to help the king." The little tailor shivered.

The princess glanced at the door. Then she stood up. "I have to go now. I told the guards my father wanted to see them. By now they have found out I was lying. They will rush back here." She hurried out of the room.

"Thanks for tipping me off!" The little tailor watched as the door shut. A few seconds later he heard the soldiers return.

The soldiers rushed into the tailor's room. "The princess is not in here." The soldiers walked out, then locked the door again.

The tailor lay on the bed of straw in the

corner. His sword was still strapped to his side. He kept his head up and his eyes open. He would be ready for the soldiers when they came back to carry out the king's plan.

The little tailor would have a plan of his own! He just hadn't figured out what it would be yet.

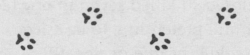

In the middle of the night, the tailor's door started to open slowly.

The brave little tailor put his head down and rolled onto his side. When the guards tip-toed into his room, he made snoring noises. He closed his eyes.

"He's sound asleep," a soldier whispered.

The brave little tailor twitched and snored. He tossed and turned. He mumbled and snored louder.

The soldiers crept nearer.

The tailor mumbled some more. "Yes, yes!" His words became clearer. But his eyes stayed closed. "I killed seven in one blow!" he growled, still pretending to be asleep.

The soldiers came nearer still.

"And I also killed two giants at once!" the tailor half-snored, half-snarled. "Why would I worry about the king . . . or his men? I could fight them all even if I was dog-tired."

"Oh!" The soldiers gasped and jumped back. Turning quickly, they ran out the door.

The brave little tailor opened his eyes. He spotted the back side of the king as the ruler disappeared out the door.

So, the top dog himself came to capture me! The brave little tailor laughed as he heard footsteps clatter down the hall. The door to the room had been left open. "Scaredy cats!" He trotted out. The king and his soldiers were already out of sight.

The brave little tailor searched up and

down the hall. He finally found a room with a real bed. There he slept peacefully until the sun came up.

The tailor stretched and shook himself awake. Then he went to find the king. The king was in his special room, sitting on his throne.

"I have a bone to pick with you," barked the brave little tailor.

The king jumped up in surprise when he heard the tailor. He looked as worried as a cat stuck in a tree. "I will sign the papers to give you half my kingdom. With your own kingdom, you can be a king. And you are free to marry my daughter."

The little tailor flipped in the air. "Cool. I'm going to be a king! We'll have a garden wedding, and . . . oh, there is one more thing." The brave little tailor wagged his tail.

"What is that?" The king had fear in his eyes.

The tailor trotted over to the throne and rested a paw on it. "I want this big red chair as a wedding present."

Looking relieved, the king sighed. "All right—it's yours."

"Thank you!" The brave little tailor turned and left the room. He walked outside to sniff out his half of the kingdom.

"Good dirt, big trees, and I haven't seen one cat. What more could a new king ask for?" He wagged his tail. "I know! A queen who digs the same things I do!"

The following week, the brave little tailor and the princess were married. They had a beautiful garden wedding. All their guests dug in and had a fun time—except for the defeated king.

The brave little tailor loved his big red chair. He and the princess, who was now a queen, lived happily ever after.

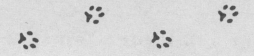

The brave little tailor was smart and believed in himself to the very end.

Speaking of the end, Joe is so far behind in the basketball game. I'm not sure he'll be able to catch up. One more basket for Stretch, and he'll be the winner. Come on, Joe!

Chapter Ten

And the Winner Is . . .

Joe had missed his two foul shots. Now it was Stretch's ball.

"Time in!" A.J. called.

Stretch dribbled the ball into play. Wishbone looked back at Joe's brown ball. It was still rolling closer to the thorn bushes. The puppy knew he had to stop it. "I can do this. I can do this. I can do this." Wishbone charged down to the ball. With a quick leap and turn, he jumped in front of the ball.

Bonk! The ball knocked him back on his tail. But the brown basketball had stopped rolling.

"I did it!" The puppy stood up. He stared at the ball. "Stay!" he ordered in his deepest voice.

Wishbone raced back up to the basketball court.

"Hey!" The terrier was surprised to see Sam and David. "When did you get here?"

Sam and David were too busy watching the game to answer. Joe had planted himself between Stretch and the basket.

"I know that look, Joe," Wishbone said. "You're worried." He watched Stretch dribble the ball. "I don't blame you. Stretch is getting ready to take another shot. You just have to squeeze in somewhere and get control of the ball."

All of a sudden, Joe ran at Stretch. He ducked under Stretch's hand, grabbing the ball as he went. Joe spun, jumped, and shot. The ball rolled around the rim. Then it dropped through the net.

"How did you do that?" Stretch asked.

Joe looked surprised. "I don't know."

"But you did it!" Sam called. She high-fived David.

"Good going, Joe," David said.

"And that's *my* boy," Wishbone bragged with pride to A.J.

"The score is Stretch four, Joe two," A.J. called. "The ball goes to Stretch."

Stretch took a firm hold on the ball. Then A.J. called time in.

"Don't let him get off a shot, Joe," David said to his friend.

"Steal the ball!" Sam called.

Wishbone gasped. "Sam, you're telling Joe to steal? I'm shocked!"

All of a sudden, Stretch charged toward the basket. Joe raised his hands up higher. He leaned left, right, then left again.

Stretch leaned the way that Joe *wasn't* leaning. He tried to step around Joe. But Joe blocked him. When Stretch tried to go the other way, his long legs tangled. One foot flew out from under him.

In an instant, Joe reached out and he snatched the ball away.

"Shoot it!" Wishbone called.

Joe pushed the ball off his fingertips. It

rose in a wide arc, then fell through the net. "All right!" Joe grinned.

"Way to go, Joe!" Wishbone ran in a circle around Sam, David, and A.J.

Sam and David smiled at each other.

"It's four to four," A.J. announced.

"But Stretch gets the ball again." Wishbone stood by David. "He has first chance at another shot."

"Time in, guys," A.J. called when Joe and Stretch were ready to play.

Stretch bounced the ball toward Joe and the basket. He tossed off a quick shot, taking Joe by surprise.

Wishbone sucked in his breath. "Oh, no, Joe!"

The ball hit the backboard, then bounced off. Joe jumped for the ball and pulled it down in midair. Stretch was right beside him. Stretch stood between Joe and the basket. Joe could not shoot.

Then Joe spun on one foot toward A.J. "Catch!" He started to throw the basketball to A.J. Stretch leaned over Joe to knock down his pass.

Wishbone cocked his head. "Joe, A.J.'s not playing!"

But Joe had been faking. Before Stretch knew he had been faked out, Joe spun around and released a hook shot. The ball bounced off the rim and sank into the net.

"I did it!" Joe jumped for joy.

"Joe-the-kid wins!" A.J. announced. "Six to four."

Wishbone flipped. "Whoo-hoo!" He looked at A.J. "I'm teaching Joe everything I know."

Joe was grinning as Wishbone and the others hurried onto the court.

"Way to go, Joe!" David nudged him with an elbow.

Joe raised his eyebrows. "Thanks. After missing all those shots, I didn't think I could ever win." He glanced down the court. "I'll be right back."

Joe got the basketball and then walked over to Stretch.

"Nice game," Joe said. "Thanks for giving me a chance to play." Smiling, he handed the ball to Stretch. "That behind-the-back move you have is really something."

Stretch finally grinned. "Yeah?"

Joe nodded. "Maybe someday I'll learn how to do it."

"Maybe." Stretch looked at his watch. "Come on, A.J. I've got to go." He started to walk off the court. Then he turned and looked over his shoulder at Joe. "Maybe you'll be up here tomorrow morning when I'm having my practice session."

"For sure!" Joe called back.

Sam smiled. "Cool, Joe. Now, how about a game of horse?" She glanced around in the grass. "Where's *your* ball?"

"Heh-heh. Funny you should ask." Wishbone walked over and looked down toward the ditch. "There it is—safe and sound," he barked.

"What's with Wishbone?" Joe asked, as he, Sam, and David went over to him. "Hey, there's my ball." Joe pointed. "How did it get down there?" Joe made his way down the hill to get the ball.

"Well . . . it's like this," Wishbone said, as he followed Joe down after the ball. "I was really, really, really excited when you got a point and—"

"If only Wishbone could talk"—Joe picked up his ball—"I'm sure he would tell us."

"Joe, I *can* talk! And I *am* telling you." Wishbone watched the kids head onto the basketball court. "But you're not listening."

"I think it's David's turn to be first." Joe passed the ball to him.

"Helllooo!" Finally, Wishbone sighed. He trotted over to the shade and looked for a good place to rest. "When I'm bigger, I just *know* they will listen to me!" He lay down in the grass. "Coaching is hard work." He put his head on his paws. "Joe, you are on your own, buddy. The coach is taking time out for a cat nap. Uh . . . make that a puppy nap!"

About "The Brave Little Tailor"

"The Brave Little Tailor" is one of many fairy tales written by Jakob and Wilhelm Grimm. It was a story someone told to them out loud, and then they wrote it down. Next they put it in a book. The stories in their books came from many different people in Germany, where the brothers lived.

One woman whom they especially listened to was the wife of a tailor. Perhaps it was this woman, the tailor's wife, who told the story of the brave little tailor to the Grimm brothers.

Jakob Grimm and Wilhelm Karl Grimm really were brothers. They were born in Germany. Jakob was the older one (1785–1863). Wilhelm was a year younger (1786–1859).

The Grimm brothers were very smart. They wrote one of the very first dictionaries! Jakob and Wilhelm also collected German folk tales. Folk tales are stories that are handed down among the regular working people. At that time, people told stories to one another while they worked. It helped to pass the time. They also told stories after work, while sitting around the fire at home. A mother would tell her children a story that she had heard as a child. Those children would grow up and tell the story to *their* children. Then those children would grow up and tell the story to *their* children. The stories are so old that no one really knows who told them in the beginning!

Some people, who thought they were better than the common people, did not think much of these stories. But Jakob and Wilhelm thought the stories were important. They thought the stories showed how the German people felt about right and wrong. So the brothers wrote the stories down on paper, just the way they were told. They knew this was a way to save them.

The Grimm brothers' first book of tales was published in 1812. It was a big hit with readers. The stories have been translated into many different languages and are still popular today.

About Vivian Sathre

Vivian Sathre is not a princess or a giant. She's not a tailor, either. And she doesn't think she's very brave. But she chose to write *The Brave Little Tailor* for WISHBONE because it is one of the fairy tales she enjoyed as a child.

When Vivian first started writing, her books were for adults. Soon she switched to writing stories for children. She was hooked right away because it was so much fun. She now believes that she will always write for children.

During the past fifteen years, Vivian has written many books. Five of those are WISH-BONE titles: *Digging Up the Past, Dog Overboard!, Wishbone's Dog Days of the West, Stage Invader,* and *Hansel and Gretel.* She also has a short story in *Tails of Terror,* a spooky collection of Wishbone's favorite Halloween tales.

Vivian loves both dogs and writing, so she has a lot of fun working for the WISHBONE series. When she isn't writing, Vivian enjoys going to baseball games, basketball games, and plays. She also enjoys doing school visits, and she gets to read her stories to the children!

Vivian lives in the Seattle area with her husband, Roger. Their two sons, Mitchell and Karsten, live there, too. They have two cats— Rocky and Eve.